Inside the Circle

Jen Jones

Photography by Jen Jones

Dedication

This book is dedicated to my children and my nephew. They are five amazing young people who have inspired me everyday , to try and be a better person. Simon, Bekah, Abby, Ansel and Jessica are my muses.

Acknowledgements

The photos were all taken at the 39th annual Inter-tribal, Pow Wow in Cherokee, North Carolina, July 4, 2014.
 I want to thank the community and the amazing dancers that are depicted in the photos. Being able to experience the togetherness of the event, and feel the true meaning of being part of the circle are what motivated me to put this book together.

The drums call the dancers,
To the circle.
Each of their drumsticks knows the beat.

Voices sing the stories,
Within the circle.
They know the sound of the old stories.

A tiny granddaughter jumps with both moccasins,
Inside the circle.
Her small arms soaring like an eaglet's.

A young grandson stomps his boots to the rhythm,
Inside the circle.
His headdress rising towards the sun.

Two women hop on one foot, chattering,
Inside the circle
Their bell dresses jingle, like playful crickets

A powerful warrior struts in his many eagle feathers,
Inside the circle.
He wears the feathers of his grandfather's, and those
he has earned.

A sweet mother carries her sleepy son,
Inside the circle.
Her fancy shawl wrapping him close in love

An old chief stalks forward, his shield at hand,
Inside the circle.
He is the protector of tradition, warrior for the past.

A grandmother shuffles with her eagle fan held,
Inside the circle.
Her graceful steps hindered by a limp.
We all stand for the Grandmother as she passes.

Everyone is invited to the circle to dance.
We are all relatives
We are all grandchildren
Inside the circle.

CPSIA information can be obtained
at www.ICGtesting.com
Printed in the USA
LVHW071447070619
620534LV00002B/16/P